We are the Dino Diggers – the best in Dino-Town.
We put things right when they go wrong and never let you down.

Bruno

Tyrone

Stacey

Terri

Ricky

For Morgan – RI
For Caden – CC

Bloomsbury Publishing, London, Oxford, New York, New Delhi and Sydney

First published in Great Britain in 2018 by Bloomsbury Publishing Plc
50 Bedford Square, London WC1B 3DP

www.bloomsbury.com

BLOOMSBURY is a registered trademark of Bloomsbury Publishing Plc

Text copyright © Rose Impey 2018
Illustrations copyright © Chris Chatterton 2018

A CIP catalogue record of this book is available from the British Library

ISBN 978 1 4088 7246 8

All papers used by Bloomsbury Publishing are natural, recyclable products made
from wood grown in well managed forests. The manufacturing processes
conform to the environmental regulations of the country of origin

Printed in China by Leo Paper Products, Heshan, Guangdong

1 3 5 7 9 10 8 6 4 2

DINO DIGGERS

Crane Calamity

Rose Impey   Chris Chatterton

BLOOMSBURY

LONDON OXFORD NEW YORK NEW DELHI SYDNEY

Today the Dino Diggers are building a house for Mr and Mrs Triceratops and all the little ceratops.

All the family have come to see how the build is going.
"Like clockwork," Terri Dactyl tells them, proudly.
Terri's in charge and it's her job to make sure of that.
She points to the Dino Digger's sign . . .

DINO DIGGERS

The Best in Town -
Dino Diggers
Never Let You Down

Bruno Brachiosaurus is working hard in his crane.
He waves to the little ceratops who all wave back.

But it's a very hot day and not everyone's working hard. Ricky Raptor, the new apprentice, is too busy daydreaming about one day being a proper Dino Digger driver.

Beep Beep!
Beep Beep!

"Look out, sleepyhead!"
Tyrone T. rex calls just in time.

"Nearly ran over your tail there," laughs Tyrone.
Bruno sees it all and feels a little sorry for Ricky.

At lunchtime, Bruno tells Tyrone, "You should slow down before there's an accident."

But Tyrone laughs. "Slow down? And turn into an old slowcoach like you! I don't think so."

Bruno doesn't laugh.
He thinks he could still show
these youngsters a thing or two . . .
and maybe he will.

Suddenly, there's a noise like thunder
and a huge cement mixer
rumbles on to site.

Terri blows her whistle.
"Back to work!" she squawks.
"This is a building site, not a rest
home for tired dinosaurs!"

Everyone hurries over to help spread the cement before it has time to set. Ricky wants to help, too. "I'm good with a brush," he says, but Tyrone tells him, "You stick to sweeping up rubbish."

"Maybe next time,"
says Stacey Stegosaurus,
a little more kindly.

Ricky's disappointed, but he's
excited, too, because he's never seen
a cement mixer up close before.

While everyone's busy, he climbs on to the scaffolding for an even closer look. He finds the perfect spot.

The cement goes round . . . and round . . . and round. Ricky's eyes go round . . . and round, until he starts to feel dizzy.

Suddenly, he loses his balance and slips off the scaffolding!

Oops!

"Help! Help!"
he calls.

But no one can hear him above
the rumble, rumble, rumble,
of the cement mixer.
Ricky's getting tired.
He wonders how much
longer he can hold on.

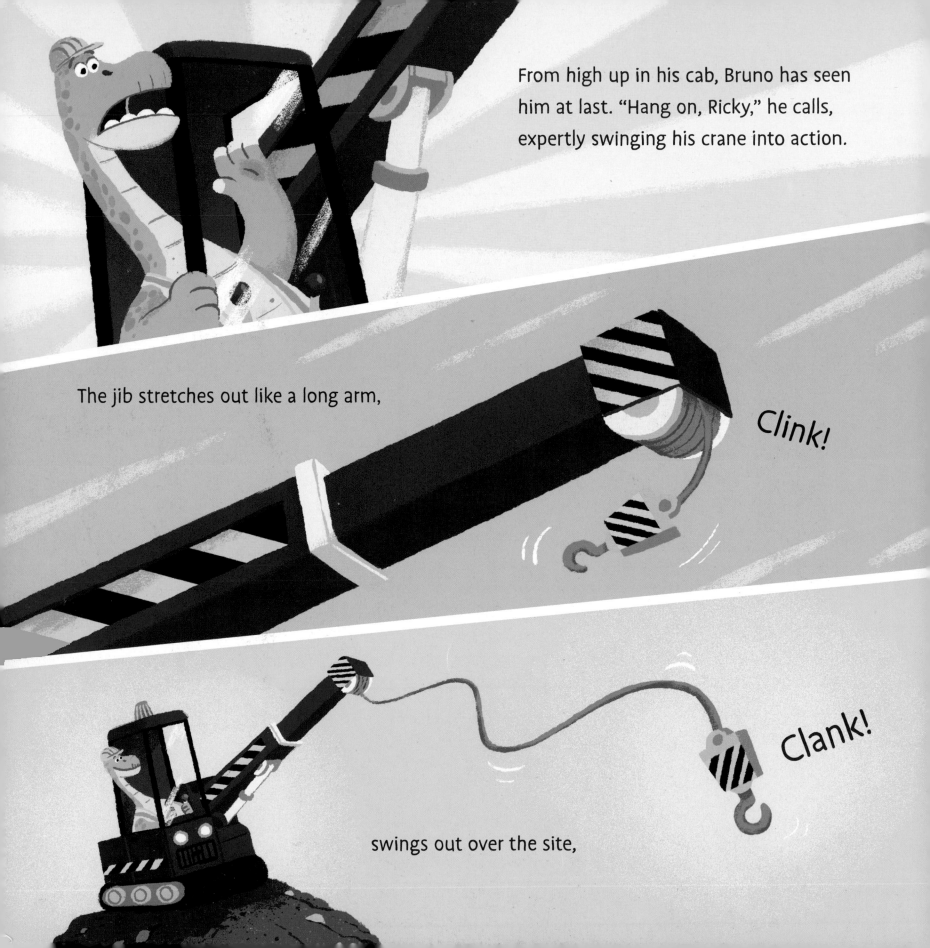

From high up in his cab, Bruno has seen him at last. "Hang on, Ricky," he calls, expertly swinging his crane into action.

The jib stretches out like a long arm,

Clink!

swings out over the site,

Clank!

and swoops down and hooks
Ricky by his overalls.

Clunk!

Then Bruno carefully lowers him to safety.
"That was quite an adventure," Tyrone tells him.
"Lucky for you Bruno was wide awake."

"Not such an old slowcoach, after all,"
says Stacey, and Tyrone agrees.

"That was a Dino-Digging delivery,
if ever I saw one," says Terri.
"Now back to work –
we've got a house to build!"

When the work's all done everyone's happy.
"Three cheers for Bruno!" they all cry, and Bruno smiles,
proud to be a Dino Digger, because . . .

The Dino Diggers Never Let You Down!

Hooray for the Dino Diggers, another job well done!
Here are other stories full of Dino-Digging fun.

Digger Disaster

Crane Calamity

Dumper Truck Danger